Tellytastic Winnie

LAURA OWEN & KORKY PAUL

Helping your child to read

Before they start

★ Talk about the back cover blurb. What does your child think Winnie might rescue the dragon from?

★ Look at the picture on the front cover. Does it give your child any clues about what might happen in the stories?

During reading

★ Let your child read at their own pace – don't worry if it's slow. They could read silently, or read to you out loud.

★ Help them to work out words they don't know by saying each sound out loud and then blending them to say the word, e.g. *f-r-o-g-sp-a-w-n, frogspawn*.

★ If your child still struggles with a word, just tell them the word and move on.

★ Give them lots of praise for good reading!

After reading

★ Look at page 48 for some fun activities.

Contents

OXFORD

UNIVERSITY PRESS

Great Clarendon Street, Oxford OX2 6DP
Oxford University Press is a department of the University of Oxford.
It furthers the University's objective of excellence in research, scholarship,
and education by publishing worldwide. Oxford is a registered trade mark
of Oxford University Press in the UK and in certain other countries

"Winnie the Bold" was first published in *Winnie the Bold* 2015
"Wilbur's Got Talent" was first published in *Winnie's Alien Sleepover* 2015
This edition published 2019

The moral rights of the author/illustrator have been asserted

Database right Oxford University Press (maker)

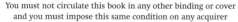

British Library Cataloguing in Publication Data

Data available

ISBN: 978-0-19-276915-2

1 3 5 7 9 10 8 6 4 2

Printed in China

Paper used in the production of this book is a natural,
recyclable product made from wood grown in sustainable forests.
The manufacturing process conforms to the environmental
regulations of the country of origin.

Acknowledgements
With thanks to Catherine Baker for editorial support

Winnie
the Bold

⭐ Chapter One ⭐

Winnie heard a noise. **Crackle! Clunk!**

"Oh no!" yelled Winnie. She jumped up, sending Wilbur flying through the air. "The TV's broken! Drat and double drat! That film was better than a cup of hot frogspawn. But now we can't watch it, Wilbur!"

Wilbur yawned.

"Did you see those children in the film, Wilbur?" said Winnie. "They went into a wardrobe and they came out in a different land! There were witches and lions, just like you and me!"

Suddenly, Winnie had an idea. "Oooh, Wilbur," she said. "Let's have our own TV adventure!"

Wilbur wasn't keen on that plan. But
Winnie grabbed him and dashed upstairs to
her bedroom. She opened the wardrobe and
pushed through her clothes. **Swish-swoosh.**
She stepped inside and suddenly . . .

. . . Winnie and Wilbur were in a
different land!

"Yikes in tights," said Winnie. "There's
a funny tin man riding a horse!" A knight
on a black horse was galloping past them.
Another knight came up to them with a
big grey horse. He thought Winnie was a
knight, too!

"Here is your horse, sir," said the knight
to Winnie.

Winnie looked up at the horse. "Slithering lizards!" she said. "It's a bit big! How am I going to ride it, Wilbur?"

Wilbur held out his paws like a step, and Winnie climbed on to the horse's back.

Then Wilbur jumped up, too.

Winnie waved her wand. "**Abracadabra!**"

★ Chapter ★
Two

At once, Winnie and Wilbur were dressed
in armour. A crowd had gathered to
watch. Then the king arrived to keep an
eye on everyone.

Winnie held on tight to the horse.
Wilbur dug his claws in.

Neigh! The horse started to gallop.

Thuddery-thud! Winnie and Wilbur were still clinging on. The knight on the black horse charged towards them. He was waving a big pointy stick. "How rude!" said Winnie. "**Abracadabra!**"

Suddenly, Winnie's wand was big, too. **CRASH!** It hit the other knight's armour.

"He's bent my wand!" yelled Winnie. "**Abracadabra!**"

Now there were sparks coming from Winnie's wand. **Kerboom!**

It made such a loud noise that the knight and the black horse ran away. "Hooray!" cheered the crowd.

Trumpets were playing as Winnie and Wilbur got down off their horse. **Parp! CRASH!**

They were heroes! This was more exciting than anything that happened on TV!

The king invited Winnie and Wilbur to lunch.

"Next, bold knight, you must go and rescue my daughter, the princess!" said the king to Winnie.

"Rescue her from what, your kinginess?" asked Winnie. She tried to post food through her helmet as if it were a letter box. **Munch!**

"From the dragon!" said the king.

Splutter! Out came the food that Winnie had posted. "*Dragon?*" said Winnie.

Wilbur tried to hide under the table.

"Yes, the dragon's cave is that way." The king pointed. "Off you go."

★ Chapter ★
Three

Winnie and Wilbur went to the dragon's
cave. **Clank-clank-clank.**

"This is as scary as a hairy fairy!" said
Winnie. "But we must save that poor
little princess!"

"Leave me alone!" cried a voice from
inside the cave.

"Come on, Wilbur!" said Winnie. They ran inside.

It was very dark, but a sudden flare of light showed the princess. It looked as if she was fighting something. "The light must be coming from the dragon's fire breath!" said Winnie to Wilbur.

"Let her go, you bully," shouted Winnie. She tried to hit the dragon with her wand. **Thump!**

"Ouch!" yelled the voice that they'd heard earlier. It wasn't coming from the princess.

"**Abracadabra!**" went Winnie, and her wand lit up the whole cave.

Suddenly, Winnie saw the dragon. It was not much bigger than Wilbur. It was holding on to a rock, and the princess was pulling its tail.

"I want a pet dragon, but this one's being naughty! It won't come with me! Waaah!" the princess wailed.

Wilbur put his paw over her mouth.

Winnie looked at the dragon. "This isn't how it works on TV!" said Winnie. "Dragons don't get bossed around by princesses. So what happened, little dragon?" she asked.

"I was in my cave minding my own business when *she* came along!" The little dragon pointed at the princess. "She is trying to dragon-nap me but I don't want to go with her."

"Mmmnbbfff," said the princess.

"You can take your paw off the princess's mouth now, Wilbur," said Winnie.

"Meeow," said Wilbur, hurrying away from the princess.

"I wanted an adventure!" said the princess. "I thought dragon-hunting would be exciting . . . but this dragon is boring!"

"I've had an idea!" said Winnie. "You can swap with me and be a knight! Knights have lots of adventures. Then Wilbur and I can go and find a wardrobe to take us home."

"Can I come home with you?" the little dragon asked Winnie.

"Why not?" said Winnie. She waved her wand. "**Abracadabra!**"

Suddenly, Winnie looked like a princess, the princess looked like a knight, and Wilbur and the dragon looked like themselves.

"Right. There must be a wardrobe in the castle," said Winnie.

"Yes," said the princess-knight. "It's in Daddy's – I mean, the king's dressing room. I'll show you!"

Back at the castle, Winnie and Wilbur and the little dragon climbed into the wardrobe. They sank straight through the soft cloaks that smelled of mothballs. And suddenly . . .

. . . they were safely back home!

For tea they had yummy marshmallows, toasted by the little dragon. Then they settled down to watch TV with a lovely cup of hot frogspawn to drink.

"Ah, a feast fit for a king!" said Winnie.

"Meeow!" said Wilbur.

"Or for witches and cats and dragons!"

"Have you got a cave for me to live in?" asked the little dragon.

"Yes," said Winnie. "There's a lovely cave in those woods out there. And there are no annoying princesses!"

Winnie and Wilbur waved the dragon goodbye. Then they went to bed.

Good knight, Winnie the Bold!

Wilbur's
Got Talent

✦ Chapter ✦
One

Wilbur was hungry. He opened the fridge door, but there was only a mouldy carrot, a bottle of lumpy milk, and a maggot. Wilbur shut the door again.

"I'm sorry, Wilbur," said Winnie. "Perhaps there's some food in the cupboard."

But the cupboard was empty, too, except for spiders' webs.

"Look!" said Winnie. "What's that at the back of the cupboard?"

It was an old can. The label said "Fancy Nancy Food for Fussy Cats".

Wilbur stuck out his tongue and made a disgusted face. "Mee-yuk!" said Wilbur.

"Oh dear," said Winnie. "You don't like this sort of food, do you, Wilbur?"

"Meeow!"

"I thought I'd got rid of all those cans ages ago!" said Winnie. "Still, this is the only food we've got left. You're going to have to eat it anyway, Wilbur."

"Meeow!"

Wilbur was so hungry that he grabbed a tin opener and opened the can.

Clank! Wind-wind-ping!

Up popped the lid and an awful pong came out of the can. Wilbur put a clothes peg on his nose, and got ready to tuck in. But just then . . .

"Oh, Wilbur! Look!" yelled Winnie, waving the lid of the can. It had a golden paw print on it. "You've won a prize, Wilbur!" said Winnie. "This golden paw print means that you are going to star in a TV advert for Fancy Nancy Food for Fussy Cats!"

Wilbur grinned a big cheesy grin. He took the clothes peg off his nose and smoothed down his fur.

Winnie pulled her phone from her pocket. "I'll ring the food people straight away!" she said. "Oooh, you'll be rich and famous, Wilbur!"

Soon a posh car stopped outside the house. The driver opened the car door, and Wilbur got inside.

The driver tried to shut the door, but Winnie pushed her way in, too. "I'm Mr Wilbur's manager," she said, trying not to bend her hat too much as she sat on the back seat.

Winnie and Wilbur waved at everyone, and drank lemonade with posh straws.

"Oooh, this is fun!" said Winnie.

★ Chapter ★ Two

At the TV studio, a make-up lady washed Wilbur's fur. Then she trimmed him and brushed him.

"Wilbur hates being washed!" said Winnie. But Wilbur gave her a look from the mirror that made her be quiet.

Lots of people gave Wilbur treats. But Winnie was left all on her own.

A man with a clipboard spoke to Wilbur. "We will start filming the advert now, sir. All you have to do is eat this bowl of Fancy Nancy Food for Fussy Cats."

"But Wilbur doesn't like that cat food!" said Winnie.

"Why don't you go home now, witchy lady?" said the man with the clipboard. "We don't need you here."

"Oh!" said Winnie. "Well, I don't want to embarrass you, Wilbur. Shall I just go home, then?"

Wilbur didn't say a thing. So Winnie went home on the bus, all by herself. Through the bus window, she saw a man putting up a huge poster of . . .

"That's Wilbur!" said Winnie to everyone on the bus. "Oooh, isn't he handsome? He's *my* cat, you know!"

Winnie felt very lonely when she got home, even though she was proud of Wilbur. And she started to worry when she looked around her house.

"Oh dear," she said. "I don't think this house is smart enough for Wilbur now. I'd better make it look smarter."

So Winnie waved her wand back and forth. "**Abracadabra!**"

At once, her house changed. Instead of being scruffy and comfortable, it was clean and smart. And Winnie was smart, too.

Smart Winnie sat in a smart chair and switched on her *huge* smart television. And guess what she saw?

"Wilbur!"

There was Wilbur trying to eat some Fancy Nancy Food for Fussy Cats.

"Oh, Wilbur, I can see you don't like it!" said Winnie to the television screen. "Oh, I can't stand this any longer. I'm coming to get you, Wilbur!"

★ Chapter ★ Three

Winnie jumped on her broomstick and flew straight to the TV studio. She waved her wand. "**Abracadabra!**"

At once, Winnie had a pinny on. She knew no one would stop her if she pretended to be a cleaner. She swept the floors of all the rooms in the studio.

At last, she heard a tiny, sad, "Meeow!"

"Wilbur!" said Winnie.

She zoomed through the door. There was
Wilbur, sitting all by himself, with a huge
pongy bowl of Fancy Nancy Food for
Fussy Cats.

"MEEOW!" shouted Wilbur, and he jumped into Winnie's arms.

Just then, they heard footsteps coming closer. **Clack-clack!**

"Hurry!" said Winnie, and she and Wilbur jumped on to the broom. They zoomed out of the window and all the way home.

Back at home, Wilbur looked around in surprise.

"I wanted to make everything smart for you," said Winnie. "Do you like our clean and smart house, Wilbur?"

"Mee-yuk!" said Wilbur, looking for a mouse to chase.

"Oh, thank goodness!" said Winnie. "I prefer our scruffy old house, too. And scruffy old me and you."

She waved her wand. "**Abracadabra!**"
Winnie and Wilbur both went back
to normal.

Winnie looked in the fridge. "I'll make
us a maggot and mouldy carrot milkshake
for tea," she said. And she threw the tin of
Fancy Nancy Food for Fussy Cats in the bin.

After reading activities

Quick quiz

See how fast you can answer these questions! Look back at the stories if you can't remember.

1) In "Winnie the Bold", how does Winnie win the contest against the knight on the black horse?
2) In "Wilbur's Got Talent", how does Winnie know that Wilbur has won the competition?
3) In "Wilbur's Got Talent", how does Winnie rescue Wilbur from the TV studio?

1) she makes a loud noise and the knight's horse runs away; 2) she finds a golden paw print on Wilbur's tin of cat food; 3) they fly out through the window on Winnie's broomstick

Try this!

★ Poor Wilbur doesn't like Fancy Nancy Food for Fussy Cats. Draw an advert for a new type of cat food that Wilbur would love.